Clarinet Exam Pieces

ABRSM Grade 4

Selected from the 2014–2017 syllabus

Name

Date of exam

CW00349688

CD

Clarinet & Piano | Piano only

Contents

Footnotes: Anthony Burton

Other pieces for Grade 4

First published in 2013 by ABRSM (Publishing) Ltd, a wholly owned subsidiary of ABRSM, 24 Portland Place, London W1B 1LU, United Kingdom © 2013 by The Associated Board of the Royal Schools of Music

Unauthorized photocopying is illegal All rights reserved. No part of this publication may be reproduced, recorded or transmitted in any form or by any means without the prior permission of the copyright owner.

Music origination by Julia Bovee Cover by Kate Benjamin & Andy Potts Printed in England by Halstan & Co. Ltd, Amersham, Bucks. Reprinted in 2013

FSC MIX Paper from responsible sources FSC™ C109619

A:1

Minuet and Trio

Third movement from Divertimento in B flat, K. 439b/Anh. 229 No. 4

Arranged by Paul Harris

W. A. Mozart
(1756–91)

The great Austrian composer Wolfgang Amadeus Mozart wrote a good deal of music for wind instruments. Much of this is in the form of serenades and divertimentos for large ensembles, of six to thirteen players, with most of the instruments in pairs. But in the mid-1780s, he composed a series of 25 short pieces for three basset horns (alto clarinets), probably for the clarinettist Anton Stadler to play with colleagues at the house of Mozart's Viennese friend Gottfried von Jacquin. The pieces fall neatly into five five-movement divertimentos, and were published in 1803, a dozen years after Mozart's death, in a version for two basset horns and bassoon. They are now well known in an edition for two clarinets and bassoon, and have also been arranged for piano under the title of 'Viennese Sonatinas'. This is an arrangement for clarinet and piano of the third piece in the fourth divertimento, a movement in the mince rhythm of the minuet with a contrasting central section or 'Trio'.

Durch die Wälder, durch die Auen

A:2

from *Der Freischütz*

Arranged by Peter Wastall

C. M. von Weber
(1786–1826)

Durch die Wälder, durch die Auen Through the woods, through the meadows; **Der Freischütz** The Freeshooter

The German composer Carl Maria von Weber composed concert music, including two concertos and other pieces for the clarinet, but is best known for his operas. *Der Freischütz*, produced in Berlin in 1821, is often described as the first German Romantic opera, with its forest setting and its story of the supernatural. The forester Max, hoping to win a shooting contest and with it the hand of his beloved Agathe, is persuaded to enter into a pact with a demonic spirit to endow his bullets with magic. In the first part of his Act I aria 'Durch die Wälder, durch die Auen', he sings of his dreams of happier times when he used to go 'through the woods, through the meadows, with a light heart'. In this arrangement, the clarinet plays the vocal line and, at the end, the woodwind instruments' repetition of the singer's first phrase.

A:3

Waltz

Op. 54 No. 1

Arranged by Peter Kolman

Antonín Dvořák
(1841–1904)

The Czech composer Antonín Dvořák wrote many pieces in dance rhythms: often in the rhythms of the folk dances of his native country and its neighbours, as in the Slavonic Dances for piano duet or orchestra, but sometimes in the internationally popular genre of the Viennese waltz. This is the first of a set of eight waltzes for piano which Dvořák composed in the winter of 1879–80; it is also one of two which he arranged at the same time for string quartet (though they are often performed by string orchestras). In its original version, the lilting main melody alternates with two episodes at faster tempos: this arrangement omits the first of those episodes, and shortens the second.

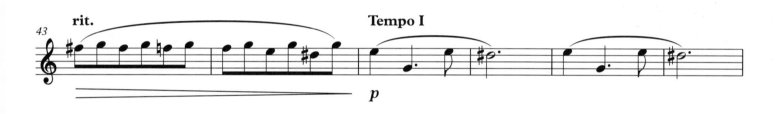

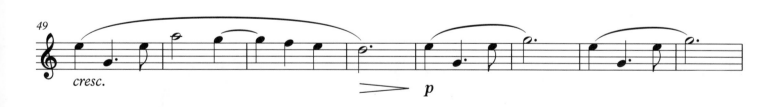

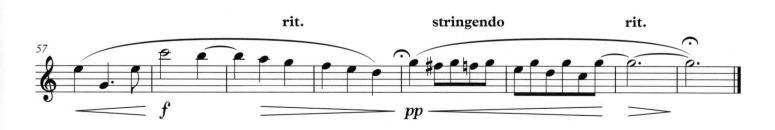

9 June. Staccatos crisp short accents
high notes lip up to keep in tune

B:1

Hernando's Hideaway

from *The Pajama Game*

Arranged by Robert Ramskill

Richard Adler (1921–2012) **and** Jerry Ross (1926–55)

Forte's louder

Tempo di tango ♩ = 120

'Hernando's Hideaway' is a song from the 1954 American musical *The Pajama Game*, with music and lyrics by Richard Adler and Jerry Ross. Adler recalled that one of the authors of the 'book' (the spoken text from the show) had asked for 'a song that can be performed in a dimly lit, smoke-filled nightclub with a lot of fervent-looking people. Oh, and make it Latin.' The result was a number that became a hit recording when it was new, and has been recorded many times by different singers and bands. It is in the metre of the tango, a dance which originated in Argentina but became popular throughout the Spanish-speaking world. The treatment is humorous, parodying the clichés of tango style: so the song should be played with exaggerated emphasis on the upbeats and on the pairs of notes at the ends of phrases, for example in bar 10, which in the song are sung to the exclamation 'Olé'. This arrangement by Robert Ramskill is reproduced from his book *Latin Connections for Clarinet* (published by Brass Wind).

B:2

Andante pacifico con rubato

Third movement from Sonatina

Paul Harris

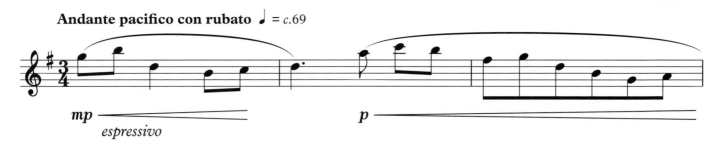

Paul Harris studied clarinet, piano, composition and conducting at the Royal Academy of Music in London, and music education at the University of London. He soon decided he would prefer teaching to performing, and he is now a greatly respected clarinet teacher, examiner and adjudicator. He has co-authored biographies of the composers Sir Malcolm Arnold, Malcolm Williamson and Sir Richard Rodney Bennett, and has written several books and many articles about music education. As a composer, he has produced numerous educational volumes, but also a number of works suitable for concert performance. Among these is his Sonatina for clarinet and piano, which was published in 1988. The third of its four movements has a tempo marking meaning 'at a peaceful walking pace': you might imagine two people conversing on a walk together. The heading also asks for *rubato*, or rhythmic freedom: the clarinettist should take the lead in this with his or her shaping of the melodic line. The marking *a piacere* in bar 25 indicates a greater rhythmic freedom.

© Copyright 1988 by Fentone Music
Used by permission. All enquiries about this piece, apart from those directly relating to the exams, should be addressed to De Haske Hal Leonard BV, Businesspark Friesland-West 15, 8466 SL Heerenveen, The Netherlands.

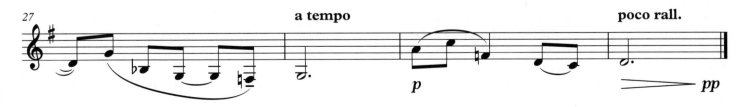

B:3

Rumba du soir

Marie-Luce Schmitt
(born 1960)

Rumba du soir Evening Rumba

Marie-Luce Schmitt is a French clarinettist, a graduate of the Bordeaux and Paris conservatoires, and now professor of clarinet at the conservatoire in Mulhouse in eastern France, where she performs with colleagues and local amateur players. She has written educational pieces for the clarinet. *Rumba du soir*, published in 2006, is in a variant of the Cuban dance rhythm of the rumba. The melody mostly fits the rhythmic pattern maintained by the piano of 3+3+2 quavers to the bar. The composer's metronome mark is given for a dotted crotchet beat, but it may be easier to think of the tempo in crotchets.

Study in C

No. 1 from 'Akkord Studien'

from *Elementarschule für Klarinette*

Friedrich Demnitz
(1845–90)

Akkord Studien Arpeggio Studies; **Elementarschule für Klarinette** Elementary School for Clarinet

Friedrich Demnitz taught at the conservatoire in the German city of Dresden and was principal clarinettist of the Dresden court orchestra, now the celebrated Staatskapelle. His *Elementary School for Clarinet* includes a series of studies based on different arpeggios, of which this is the first. The breath marks in bars 39 and 41 are editorial.

Source: *Elementarschule für Klarinette* (Peters, n.d.)

C:2

Study in D minor

No. 10 from *21 Intermediate Studies for Clarinet*

Paula Crasborn-Mooren
(born 1959)

Paula Crasborn-Mooren was born in the Netherlands in 1959, and studied the clarinet at the Brabant conservatoire in Belgium. She is currently a performer on the instrument, and teaches it in Roermond and Thorn in the south-east of the Netherlands. She has published three books of melodic studies for the clarinet. This is a study in dynamics and tonguing, and requires even tone production across the different registers.

Jack the Lad

No. 20 from *Scaling the Heights*

Roger Purcell
(born 1954)

C:3

Roger Purcell is a performer and teacher of clarinet and saxophone, based in the north-west of England. He has written a book on advanced technique, sets of duets for clarinets and saxophones, and also *Scaling the Heights*, a collection of studies progressing from Grade 1 to Grade 8, which he hopes students will find 'challenging, rewarding and enjoyable to practise'. This study is named with the slang term for a carefree and self-assured young man – hence the tempo marking 'Confidently'.